SESAME STREET
ABBY CADABBY'S
Rhyme Time

By P.J. Shaw
Illustrated by Tom Leigh

The DALMATIAN PRESS and PIGGY TOES PRESS names and logos are trademarks of Dalmatian Publishing Group, Atlanta, Georgia 30329. No part of this book may be reproduced or copied in any form without written permission from the copyright owner. All rights reserved.

Printed in the U.S.A.
ISBN: 1-61524-338-0

10 11 12 13 B&M 35652 10 9 8 7 6 5 4 3 2
Sesame Street Handle Box Set Book: Abby Cadabby's Rhyme Time

"Lumpkin, bumpkin, diddle-diddle dumpkin, zumpkin, frumpkin, pumpkin!

As a fairy-in-training, I practice my magic tricks with rhymes—you know, words that end with the same sound, like **bat** and **cat**! Rhymes are so fun to find! I know—let's find some rhymes together. Hmmmm. What words rhyme with … **rhyme**?"

What words rhyme with **sheep**?
Noisy cars that go **"beep"**!
A ballet dancer's **leap**,
And a trash heap to **sweep**.

What words rhyme with **go**?
I bet that you **know**!
There's a boat you can **row**,
And cars that go *slooooow*.

Which words sound like **zap**?
Fairy wings going **flap**!
And the shoes that you **tap**
To the beat—as you **snap**!

Do some words rhyme with **stick**?
Yes! A house made of **brick**,
A soft baby **chick**,
Or a camera to **click**!

What rhymes with **nose**?
Snuffleupagus **toes**,
A swishy fish that **glows**!
And a slithery **hose**.

What words rhyme with **sloppy**,
Like Oscar's **Jalopy**?
Bunnies all **hoppy**
With ears that are **floppy**.

And last, what rhymes with **tabby**?
A blankie that's **shabby**,
A fairy named **Abby**,
And the family **Cadabby**!